Bo and the Merbaby

Read more
UNICORN DIARIES
books!

1

2

3

4

5

6

Unicorn Diaries

Bo and the Merbaby

Rebecca Elliott

BRANCHES

SCHOLASTIC INC.

For the Hudsons. A truly magical family. XX —R.E.

Special thanks to Kyle Reed for his contributions to this book.

Library of Congress Cataloging-in-Publication Data

Names: Elliott, Rebecca, author. | Elliott, Rebecca. Unicorn diaries ; 5.
Title: Bo and the merbaby / Rebecca Elliott.
Description: First edition. | New York : Branches/Scholastic Inc., 2021.
| Series: Unicorn diaries ; 5 | Summary: Merbaby Flo was born with only one fin, unable to swim–so Bo and the other unicorns set out for the Shiny Sea to find the Golden Fish and ask Goldie to use her magic to help baby Flo.
Identifiers: LCCN 2021001215 | ISBN 9781338745542 (paperback) |
ISBN 9781338745559 (hardcover) | ISBN 9781338745566 (ebk)
Subjects: LCSH: Unicorns–Juvenile fiction. | Mermaids–Juvenile fiction. |
Magic–Juvenile fiction. | Helping behavior–Juvenile fiction. |
Diaries–Juvenile fiction. | CYAC: Unicorns–Fiction. |
Mermaids–Fiction. | Magic–Fiction. | Helpfulness–Fiction. |
People with disabilities–Fiction. | Diaries–Fiction. | LCGFT: Diary fiction.
Classification: LCC PZ7.E45812 Bl 2021 | DDC [Fic]–dc23
LC record available at https://lccn.loc.gov/2021001215

10 9 8 7 6 5 4 3 2   21 22 23 24 25

Printed in China   62
First edition, August 2021

Edited by Kait Feldmann
Book design by Marissa Asuncion

Table of Contents

Sunday

Hello again, Diary! It's me, Bo the unicorn! (My full name is Rainbow Tinseltail). I've missed you. Have you missed me?!

In case you've forgotten, I live in a magical place called Sparklegrove Forest.

Rainbow Falls

Troll Caves

Glimmer Glade

Sparklegrove School for Unicorns

Dragon Nests

Budbloom Meadow

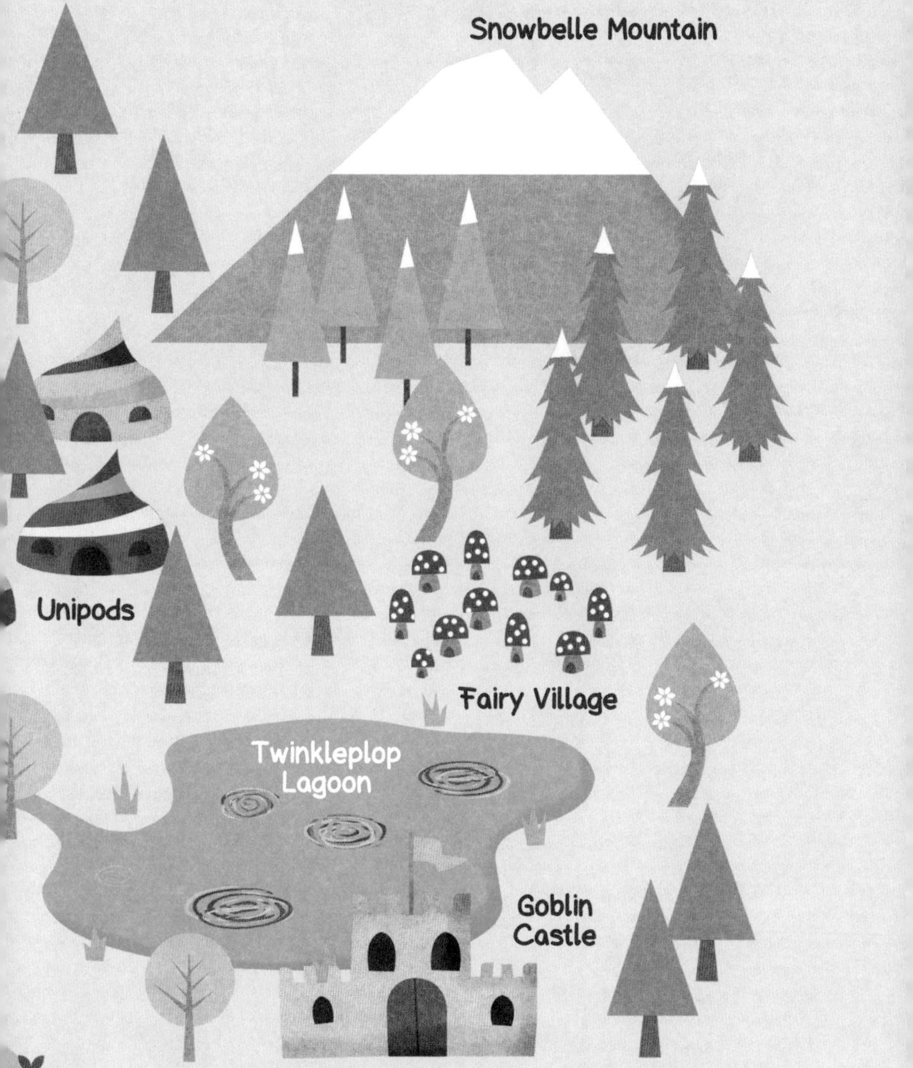

Snowbelle Mountain

Unipods

Fairy Village

Twinkleplop
Lagoon

Goblin
Castle

It's not just unicorns who live here
though . . .

Mermaids live here, too! Here are some mermaid facts for you:

They live in Twinkleplop Lagoon.

They are all female.

They swim upstream every day to hunt for food.

They can swim really well from the day they are born! New baby mermaids are very rare.

Unicorns can't swim as well as mermaids. But we can do lots of other cool stuff.

Tail
Swishing it makes our Unicorn Power work.

Mouth
When we snore, it sounds like music.

Tummy
We fill it with only brightly colored food.

Hooves
Rainbows fly out of them when we dance.

Here are some more fun **UNIFACTS**:

No two unicorns look the same.
We're all different colors!

We each have a different Unicorn
Power. I'm a Wish Unicorn. I can grant
one wish every week!

None of us were born. We just appeared on really starry nights!

Our horns can glow, which is handy for bedtime reading!

My unicorn friends and I live together in **UNIPODS**. We go to Sparklegrove School for Unicorns (S.S.U.).

Our teacher is Mr. Rumptwinkle. (Sometimes it's difficult to spot him, because he's a Shape-Shifter Unicorn!)

These are my classmates, and here are their magical powers:

Nutmeg Silvertips
Flying Unicorn

Scarlett Sugarlumps
Thingamabob Unicorn

Jed Glitterock
Weather Unicorn

Monty Dumpling
Size-Changer Unicorn

Piper Forestine
Healer Unicorn

Sunny Huckleberry
Crystal-Clear Unicorn

We learn about all sorts of subjects, like . . .

ENCHANTED PLANTS

USE OF MAGICAL POWERS

HORN CARE
(LIKE HOW TO POLISH OUR HORNS UNTIL THEY SPARKLE)

MANE AND TAIL STYLING

Every week, we try to learn or do something new. When we do, we earn a patch for our patch blanket. Once our blankets are full, we are ready to graduate.

I can't wait to see what patch we'll be trying to get this week! Good night, Diary! (I hope my musical snoring doesn't keep you awake!)

The Merbaby!

Monday

Mr. Rumptwinkle told us the most **GLITTERRIFIC** news this morning!

Good morning, class. I have just heard that a new merbaby will be born this week!

Wow!

How exciting!

AND . . . there will be a celebration! We are all invited to Twinkleplop Lagoon to meet her!

We were all SO excited about the new merbaby and the celebration!

Then things got even more exciting. Mr. Rumptwinkle told us what this week's patch will be.

He told us that to earn the patch, we need to complete three tasks:

1. Make the merbaby a gift.
2. Learn how to do a new trick in water. (We will perform in a Water Show at Twinkleplop Lagoon on Saturday!)
3. Help out a water creature.

We spent the rest of the day making our presents for the merbaby. It made us even MORE excited about meeting her.

I started knitting her a hat. Do you like it, Diary?

Before **CLOUDTIME**, Mr. Rumptwinkle trotted into our **UNIPOD**.

Good news, unicorns! The merbaby has been born! Tomorrow, we can all go to meet her and celebrate at the lagoon.

We were so excited that we could barely sleep.

I wonder what they've named her?

I wonder what color her tail is?

I can't wait to see her swim!

What a magical day, Diary! I'm so excited about tomorrow!

A Sad Tail

Tuesday

Today we carried our presents over to Twinkleplop Lagoon. Lots of other creatures were there, too. We all gathered around the water.

The merbaby's mom was sitting on a rock in the middle of the pool. She proudly showed us her baby.

Everyone! Meet Flo!

We all clapped, and Flo clapped, too. It was so sweet!

We all gave Flo the presents we'd made for her.

It was great to complete the first WATER patch task. But mostly, it was just great to see Flo so happy!

We felt so lucky that the mermaids were going to help us! Learning new water tricks is our second task!

We had such fun splashing around.
The mermaids taught us somersaults,
dives, and underwater handstands.
(Well, more like **HOOFSTANDS** for us!)

We soon got tired out. Water tricks
are hard work! Not for mermaids
though, they can swim and do tricks all
day long from the day they're born!

And Diary, that's when Flo's mermom explained something to us.

That's sweet, but don't be sad. Flo can ride on my back — like this — most of the time! The only time she can't is when I'm swimming upstream to find food.

And look at her. She's perfect just as she is.

Flo clapped, and we all cheered!

We played with Flo until the sun went down.

At **CLOUDTIME**, I couldn't sleep. Sunny was still awake, too, and we talked about how lovely Merbaby Flo is. But something was bothering me . . .

I still can't help feeling sad that she can't swim!

Me too! I just wish something could be done.

4

The Neverending Woods

Wednesday

Today we trotted to the river at Rainbow Falls. We practiced our new water tricks that the mermaids taught us.

Look at us! We're getting pretty good!

We can show Mr. Rumptwinkle our new tricks at the Water Show on Saturday!

Sunny and I looked at each other. We were thinking the same thing.

We all thought Merbaby Flo could use our help though. So we sat around trying to think up ways to help her.

I've got it! Bo could grant Flo a wish to make her tail better!

Of course! Great idea, Piper!

We told Mr. Rumptwinkle our plan.

It's a lovely idea. But you can't use unicorn magic to change the way someone was born.

Oh.

We asked Mr. Rumptwinkle if there was anything we could do.

Well, there is one very powerful and wise magical creature that might be able to help.

Who?

She's called The Golden Fish. Forest creatures have said that her magic is SUPER strong. They say she lives in the Shiny Sea, past Sparklegrove Forest.

Maybe we wouldn't be able to find her either. But then I thought — we're unicorns! We shouldn't give up!

Come on, unicorns! If anyone can find The Golden Fish, we can!

Bo's right! When we work together, we can do anything!

We packed our things and set off.

We sneaked past the troll caves.

We swam across Rainbow Falls.

And we trotted along the river. We were going farther than we'd ever been before in the forest. It was exciting but also a bit scary.

The forest was very large. We all jumped when we heard something moving in the bushes behind us.

Did you hear that?

I'm scared!

Don't worry, it was probably nothing.

When I heard another noise, I turned around. There were big red eyes staring at us from the bushes!!!

We ran as fast as we could!

But we stopped galloping when we heard a voice behind us.

We were still a bit scared. We'd never seen a werewolf before! But he sounded kind, so we waited to hear what he had to say.

But if you go that way, you'll get lost in the Neverending Woods. The Shiny Sea is the other way. Just thought you should know.

If Barry hadn't helped us, we would have gotten lost!

Thank you! Do you know if The Golden Fish is real?

Oh, she's real, all right! She hides out in a cave nearby.

We felt so happy to know we hadn't come all this way for nothing! But then Barry said something else that made us <u>not</u> so happy.

So Barry gave us his map!

Mushroom Meadow

Shiny Sea

Sparklegrove Forest

 I'm a Wish Unicorn — is there anything I could magic-up for you to say thank you?

Well, that's very kind. I do wish there were a sign in this forest, so creatures would stop getting lost!

I swished my tail and magicked-up a signpost.

SHINY SEA

SPARKLEGROVE FOREST

BARRY'S LAIR

Oh, thank you! I love it! Bye-bye, unicorns!

When we got to Mushroom Meadow, it was getting dark. We made camp for the night. Then we toasted pink marshmallows on the fire!

We've come this far, Diary — now all we can do is keep going!

5

The Golden Fish

The next morning, we set off early. Finally, we reached the Shiny Sea!

Look! It's SO pretty and twinkly!

We kept going until we reached a golden cave. This must be it!

We were very nervous as we knocked on the door of the cave.

A minute later, the door opened. We had found her – The Golden Fish! But she didn't seem happy to see us.

Go away!

She slammed the door!

We didn't go away though. We were here for Merbaby Flo. We had to stay strong for her. So we knocked again. And again.

At last, she shouted back at us from inside the cave.

There was silence for a minute. The door swung open.

We told her about the little merbaby,
Flo, who needs some help.

Goldie listened
and nodded.

We talked late into the night. Then Goldie let us sleep in her cave.

She might be super powerful, but Goldie is also super friendly. We can't wait to take her to meet Flo tomorrow!

6

Goldie Meets Flo

It was lots of fun to travel back to Twinkleplop Lagoon with a new friend. We practiced our water tricks, which Goldie loved. And sometimes she gave other creatures a lift downstream!

I haven't been out of my cave for so long. I forgot how much fun it is to swim through the forest!

When we got to the lagoon, we asked Goldie to hide. We wanted to surprise the mermaids!

But then we noticed . . .

Flo's mermom was looking upset. We asked her what was wrong.

I need to go upstream to help the other mermaids find food. But it's not safe for Flo to come with me. I can't leave her here on her own.

Don't worry! We might have found someone who can help!

Come out, Goldie!

Flo laughed and reached out to Goldie.

Flo's mermom handed Flo to Goldie.
They swam around and Flo giggled and
clapped.

Eventually, Goldie settled into the water again.

What do you think, Goldie?

Can you fix her?

Flo's mermom frowned.

Thank you for coming all this way, Goldie. But Flo doesn't need fixing. She's perfect just the way she is!

Flo giggled and blew bubbles, which made us all laugh.

Goldie turned to the unicorns.

I do see a problem that needs fixing, but it isn't Flo. And magic isn't always the key.

It was getting dark so we didn't have time to ask Goldie what she meant. The mermaids said Goldie could stay with them for the night. We said good-bye and went home to think about what Goldie had said.

We lay on our cloud beds, feeling a bit disappointed. We hadn't earned our WATER patches because we hadn't helped a water creature.

But Diary, if Goldie is right, maybe there is <u>another</u> way we can help out. We will think of something tomorrow.

The Water Show

At breakfast, we all felt a bit sad.

Cheer up, unicorns! You've had an adventure this week. You've learned new things. And I'm very proud of you for trying so hard to help Flo. It doesn't matter if you don't get your patch.

Then Mr. Rumptwinkle reminded us that we still had the Water Show to look forward to today. We couldn't wait to show the mermaids how much better we were at the water tricks they taught us!

We decided to practice our tricks one more time before the show. But . . .

Sunny wasn't done eating!

Will you hold my bowl for me while I practice my trick?

It gave Piper a really good idea!

I just realized what Goldie meant yesterday!

Tell us, Piper!

Flo never needed our help. But <u>Flo's mermom</u> did! She said she couldn't hold Flo and hunt at the same time.

You're right! It's her mermom that needs the help! Can we think of a way to help her so she can go upstream?

We came up with the best idea together! We couldn't wait to tell the mermaids. But first, it was time for the Water Show!

The Water Show was SO MUCH FUN!

Scarlett magicked-up a hoop out of her mane. Then she somersaulted through it.

Piper made her horn glow as she swam underwater.

Nutmeg flew high above the lagoon and then dived in.

Jed made it windy and then surfed on a big wave.

Monty made himself big and jumped in, splashing us all.

Sunny went invisible and surprised us all by popping out of the water.

I made rainbows come out of my hooves as I danced underwater.

Everyone clapped when our show ended. Now it was time to tell Flo's mermom our plan!

We'd like to <u>merbabysit</u> Flo whenever you need to go upstream.

That's a fantastic idea, unicorns! Thank you so much!

And we thought Goldie might like to move to Sparklegrove Forest!

Oh, I would LOVE that! I'll never be lonely again!

Great idea!

Then Goldie used her magic to bring her golden cave right next to Twinkleplop Lagoon!

Suddenly, sparkles flew all around us. We'd helped TWO water creatures and completed the final task! We earned our WATER patch!

TWINKLE-POP!

I had a great week, Diary! Do you like my new WATER patch?

And it's not even the best thing I got this week. The best part was discovering that being born different is totally okay. And we made two new watery friends along the way!

See you next time, Diary!

Rebecca Elliott may not have a magical horn or sneeze glitter, but she's still a lot like a unicorn. Rebecca always tries to have a positive attitude, she likes to laugh a lot, and she lives with some great creatures — her noisy-yet-charming children, her lovable but naughty dog Frida, and a big, lazy cat named Bernard. She gets to hang out with these fun characters and write stories for a living, so she thinks her life is pretty magical!

Rebecca is the author of several picture books, the young adult novel PRETTY FUNNY, the bestselling Unicorn Diaries early chapter book series, and the bestselling Owl Diaries series.

Unicorn Diaries

How much do you know about Bo and the Merbaby?

Reread Chapter 1. What are five fun facts about mermaids?

Why didn't Goldie want to talk to the unicorns? How do you think Goldie felt when she slammed her door?

List the water tricks each unicorn did. What water trick would <u>you</u> perform?

The unicorns realized Flo didn't need their help. Instead, they ended up helping two other water creatures. Who did they help, and how?

Think about a time <u>you</u> helped someone. What did you do? How did it make you feel?